BLAZERS

GROSS JOBS
Working with
ANIMALS
An Augmented Reading Experience
by Nikki Bruno

CAPSTONE PRESS
a capstone imprint

Blazers Books are published by Capstone Press,
1710 Roe Crest Drive, North Mankato, Minnesota 56003
www.mycapstone.com

Library of Congress Cataloging-in-Publication data
Names: Clapper, Nikki Bruno, author.
Title: Gross jobs working with animals : 4D an augmented reading experience /
  by Nikki Bruno.
Description: North Mankato, Minnesota : an imprint of Capstone Press, [2019]
  | Series: Blazers. Gross jobs 4D | Audience: Age 6-8. | Audience: Grade 4 to 6.
Identifiers: LCCN 2018036630| ISBN 9781543554892 (hardcover) | ISBN
  9781543558982 (paperback) | ISBN 9781543554953 (ebook pdf)
Subjects: LCSH: Animal specialists--Vocational guidance--Juvenile literature.
  | Zoologists--Vocational guidance--Juvenile literature.
Classification: LCC SF80 .C53 2019 | DDC 590.92--dc23
LC record available at https://lccn.loc.gov/2018036630

Editorial Credits
Hank Musolf, editor; Bobbie Nuytten, designer; Heather Mauldin,
media researcher; Katy LaVigne, production specialist

Photo Credits
Alamy: Astrid Hinderks, 26-27, Chris Howes/Wild Places, 20-21, Farlap, 19, Peter
Horree, 22-23, robertharding, 8-9, Tim Brown, 4-5; ASSOCIATED PRESS: Brian
Davies/The Register-Guard, 10-11; iStockphoto: fcafotodigital, 10 (inset), groveb, 14,
M_a_y_a, 24-25, Morsa Images, 28-29, nechaev-kon, 24 (inset), Singkham, 20 (inset);
Minden Pictures: Francois Savigny, 12-13, Kevin Schafer, 26 (inset), Pete Oxford, 12
(inset); Newscom: CHARLES BERTRAM/KRT, 15; Shutterstock: Alexey Savchuk,
16-17, cate_89, cover, 1, ESB Professional, 4 (inset), ShutterDivision, 6-7
Design Elements:
Shutterstock: Alhovik, kasha_malasha, Katsiaryna Chumakova, Yellow Stocking

Printed and bound in the United States of America.
PA48

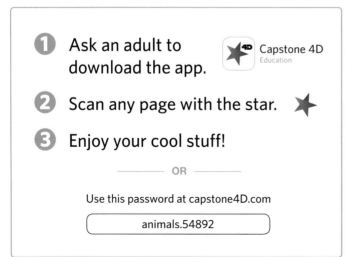

1 Ask an adult to download the app.

2 Scan any page with the star.

3 Enjoy your cool stuff!

Capstone 4D
Education

OR

Use this password at capstone4D.com

animals.54892

TABLE OF CONTENTS

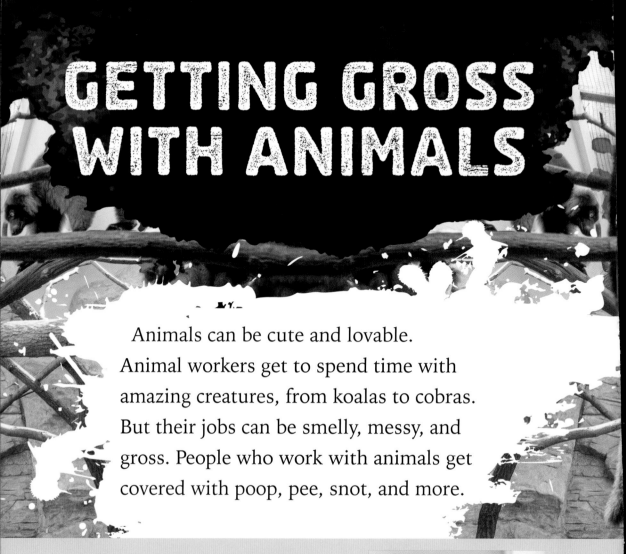

GETTING GROSS WITH ANIMALS

Animals can be cute and lovable. Animal workers get to spend time with amazing creatures, from koalas to cobras. But their jobs can be smelly, messy, and gross. People who work with animals get covered with poop, pee, snot, and more.

DID YOU KNOW?

Pet ownership is on the rise. Today about 70 percent of American households have pets. In 2009 that number was about 50 percent.

VET TECH

Vet techs help veterinarians. They check the animals' coats for ticks. They clean dirty teeth and treat **pus**-filled wounds. Vet techs also help with surgeries. They see and smell the insides of animals.

GROSS-O-METER

DID YOU KNOW?

Dogs have liquid-filled **glands** where their poop comes out. Vet techs may have to squeeze out the smelly liquid.

pus—thick yellow fluid made up of cells that fight infection

gland—an organ in the body that makes certain chemicals

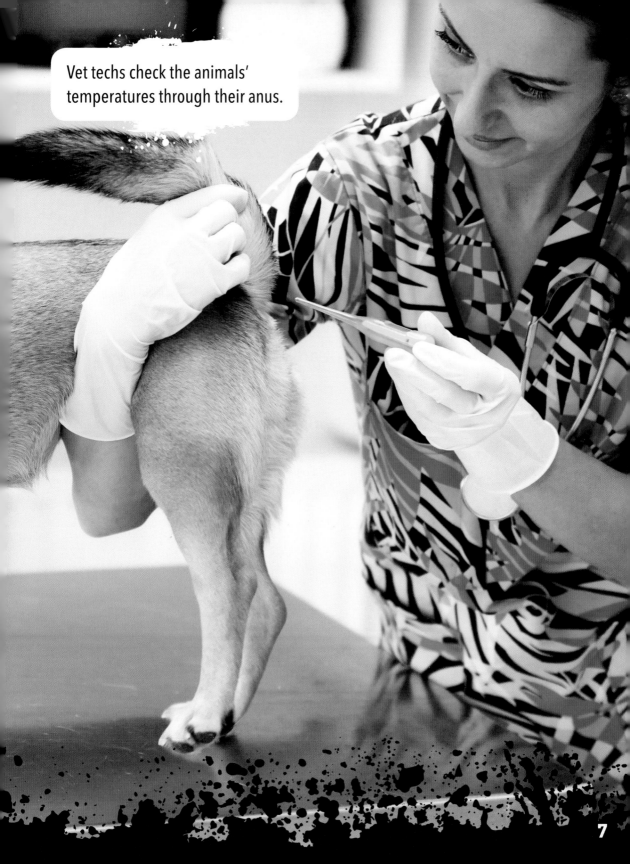

Vet techs check the animals' temperatures through their anus.

WHALE SNOT COLLECTOR

Scientists study whale snot to learn about them. Who collects this goo? Whale snot collectors do! They pick up the snot with a long pole. It's normal to get blasted by whale sneezes while getting the snot!

GROSS-O-METER

DID YOU KNOW?

Snot collection is so gross that some scientists make a **drone** do the dirty work. It is called a SnotBot.

drone—an unmanned, remote-controlled aircraft

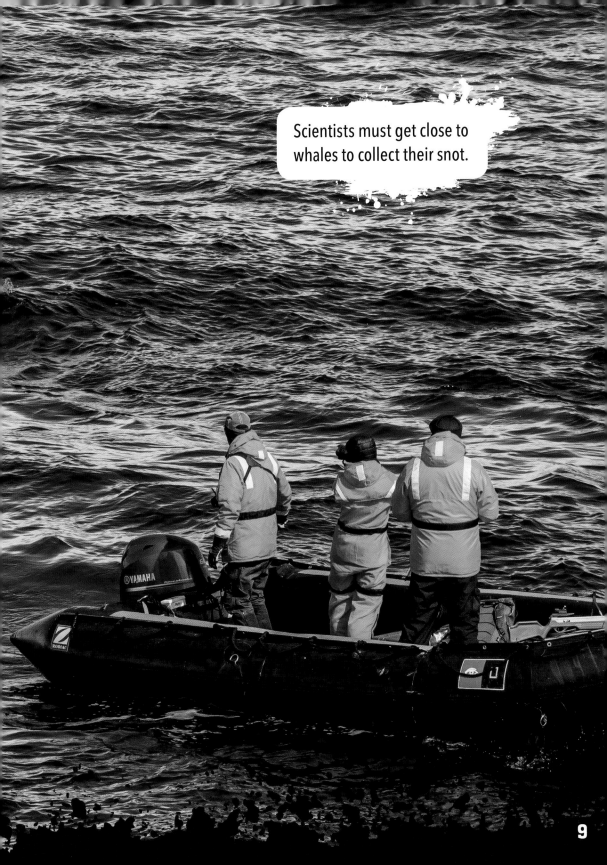

Scientists must get close to whales to collect their snot.

EXTERMINATOR

Exterminators remove pests from people's homes and businesses. They get up close to termites, rats, ants, bats, and other animals. These workers use traps and dangerous poisons. Sometimes they have to carry the pests out by hand!

GROSS-O-METER

DID YOU KNOW?

Cockroaches breathe through holes in their body. A cockroach can live for a week without its head.

exterminator—a person who rids places of unwanted pests for a living

SNAKE RESEARCHER

What's grosser than a snake? Its vomit! Snake researchers look at snake vomit to find out what snakes eat. First, they squeeze the snake to make it throw up. Then they study the vomit.

GROSS-O-METER

DID YOU KNOW?

Snakes do not want to be caught! They often pee and poop on researchers.

Snakes don't poop as often as other animals.

DEER PEE FARMER

Who in the world would want to collect deer pee? These farmers do! Deer pee farmers lead deer to a building with floors that collect pee. The pee is stored in fridges. Deer hunters use the pee as **bait** to attract male deer.

GROSS-O-METER

DID YOU KNOW?

The number of deer in Michigan is unusually high. All of the deer pee is harming Michigan's hemlock trees.

bait—food that attracts larger creatures so that they can be caught

MAGGOT FARMER

Maggots are disgusting! These squirmy, worm-like creatures are young flies. Maggot farmers **breed** and package millions of them. They sell maggots as fish bait and farm animal food.

FLESH EATERS

GROSS-O-METER

Maggots don't just look gross. They also eat gross food. Their favorites are dead animals. Flies lay their eggs on living or dead animals. After hatching, the maggots have a ready-made meal.

breed—to mate and raise a certain kind of animal

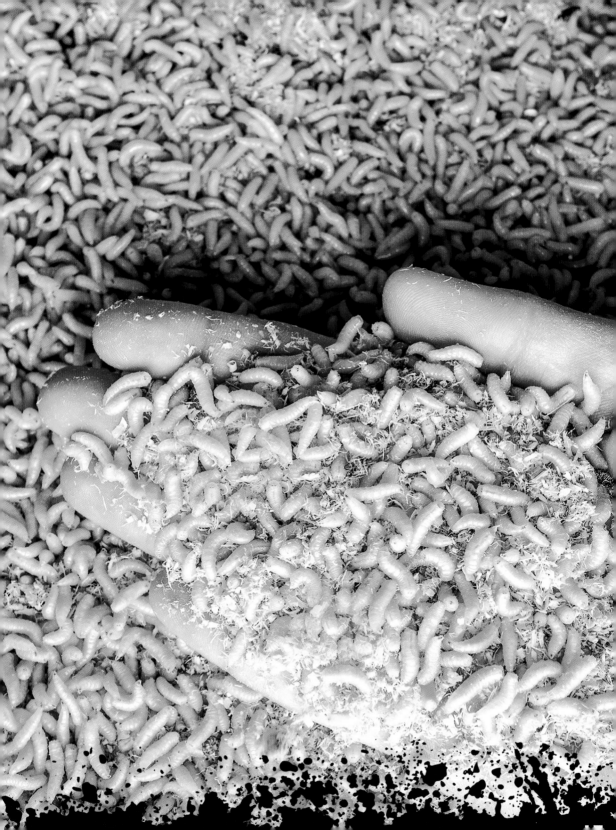

COW HOOF TRIMMER

Cow hoof trimming is a lot messier than clipping nails! Cows must be roped down on a special device. The trimmers use special tools to shave away the hooves. It's normal to get covered in cow poop in the process!

GROSS-O-METER

DID YOU KNOW?

Cow hoof trimmers don't just trim cows' hooves. They may treat sores. They may give care to cows that are having trouble walking.

GUANO COLLECTOR

Some do their jobs knee-deep in bat poop. Others scrape bird poop off rocks. These workers are called **guano** collectors. Guano is a great **fertilizer**. It also keeps pests away from plants.

GROSS-O-METER

DID YOU KNOW?

In 1850 guano was worth one-quarter the price of gold. It was one of the best fertilizers at that time.

guano—dried bird or bat droppings, used as fertilizer

fertilizer—a substance used to make crops grow better

Guano collectors often find bat poop in caves.

LEATHER TANNER

Leather is made in a messy process called tanning. First, tanners take the animals' skin off. Then they remove hair, blood, and flesh. The skin gets soaked, scraped, and sanded. Over time it becomes soft and flexible.

GROSS-O-METER

DID YOU KNOW?

Leather tanning has changed over time. Leather tanners used to use vegetables, smoke, or even animal fat to turn animal skins into leather.

DOG GROOMER

Dog groomers deal with poop, pee, fleas, drool, and dog breath. They clip nails, scrub dirt, pick off ticks, and clean out ears. They also get covered in hair.

GROSS-O-METER

DID YOU KNOW?

Groomers need to be careful when cleaning pets with fleas or ticks. The gross critters can move from the pet to the groomer!

tick

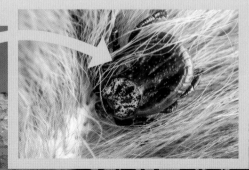

groom—to clean and make an animal look neat

ZOOKEEPER

When hundreds of wild animals live in a small area, things get dirty fast! Zookeepers shovel elephant poop. They handle raw meat and smelly fish. Animals spit and pee on zookeepers. Monkeys might even throw poop at them.

SLOTHS: THE CLEANEST POOPERS

Most animals leave their poop where it drops. Sloths spend most of their time in trees. To poop, they slowly climb down the tree. They poop on the ground. Then they neatly bury their poop in the ground. Sloths poop once a week.

HATS OFF TO ANIMAL WORKERS!

What would the world be like without animal workers? They keep our pets healthy. They keep zoos clean. They get rid of pests. They brave a lot of grossness to get their jobs done!

GLOSSARY

bait (BAYT)—food that attracts larger creatures so that they can be caught

biology (bye-AH-luh-jee)—the study of plant and animal life

breed (BREED)—to mate and raise a certain kind of animal

DNA (DEE-ehn-ay)—material in cells that gives people their individual characteristics; DNA stands for deoxyribonucleic acid

drone (DROHN)—an unmanned, remote-controlled aircraft

exterminator (ik-STUHR-muh-nay-tuhr)—a person who rids places of unwanted pests for a living

fertilizer (FUHR-tuh-ly-zuhr)—a substance used to make crops grow better

gland (GLAND)—an organ in the body that makes certain chemicals

guano (GWAH-noh)—dried bird or bat droppings, used as fertilizer

pus (PUHSS)—thick, yellow fluid made up of cells that fight infection

zoology (zoh-OL-uh-jee)—the science of studying animals

READ MORE

Duhaime, Darla. *Gross Jobs.* Gross Me Out! Vero Beach, Fla.: Rourke Educational Media, 2016.

Edgar, Sherra G. *Large Animal Veterinarian.* Gross Jobs. Mankato, Minn.: Child's World, 2015.

Gleisner, Jenna Lee. *Bug Exterminator.* Gross Jobs. Mankato, Minn.: Child's World, 2015.

INTERNET SITES

Use FactHound to find Internet sites related to this book.

Visit *www.facthound.com*

Just type in 9781543554922 and go.

Check out projects, games and lots more at
www.capstonekids.com

INDEX